The Scallop Christmas

Published by

Islandport Press

P.O. Box 10

267 U.S. Route One, Suite B

Yarmouth, Maine 04096

www.islandportpress.com

info@islandportpress.com

Text copyright © 2009 by Jane Freeberg

Illustrations copyright © 2009 by Astrid Sheckels

ISBN: 978-1-934031-25-4

Library of Congress Control Number: 2009929431

Printed in China

ISLANDPORT PRESS   YARMOUTH • MAINE

For Ernest, who listened a thousand times, and thinks I can do anything—JANE FREEBERG

For Anna, Ruth, Jacob, and Grendel—ASTRID SHECKELS

JANE FREEBERG
The Scallop

ASTRID SHECKELS

Christmas

ISLANDPORT PRESS

On Christmas Eve, as a light December snow drifted gently to the ground outside, my grandchildren and I decorated our Christmas tree. As always, I hung two painted scallop shells in a place of honor near the top. The shells were old, chipped, and dull, and to some they may have looked out of place hanging among the brightly colored glass ornaments that sparkled red and gold and blue. But to me, they were the most beautiful. My mother painted them years and years ago, and each Christmas they bring back precious memories—memories of perhaps the happiest day of my life.

It all began one fall when I was ten. My Poppa's friend, John Howard, a local fisherman, stopped by our house to tell Poppa that the scallops in our bay were ready to harvest. There was an enormous number of them, and we didn't know where they came from because we'd never seen them in our bay before. But, oh my, they were very, very welcome. In those days, times were hard and money was scarce. Most people in our village had barely enough to get by and needed every extra dollar they could earn. We knew that when the scallops were ready to harvest, fish merchants would come to our small village and pay cash for them, and then sell them to big city restaurants and other buyers.

Most of the men in our little New England fishing village were lobstermen or fishermen or farmers, but Poppa was the teacher at the one-room schoolhouse. After Mr. Howard gave us the news about the scallops, he asked Poppa for a favor.

"Lucas," he said, "we'd all be much obliged if you would close down the school for a few days so we can take all the young'uns out scalloping. The prices are awful good and folks 'round here really need the money."

According to local rules, each fisherman could sell just one bushel of scallops each day for each person in his boat, so it made good Yankee sense to take everyone possible, from Grandma to the babies. Poppa was the most popular man in town when he agreed to close school for an entire week so everyone could go scalloping.

My Poppa wasn't like most dads in town—big strong men weathered by the sun. No, Poppa was tall and skinny. He loved his vegetable garden even more than he loved his ramshackle old boat, the *Pineapple*. Once in a while when he was gardening, his tricky shoulder would act up and slip out of joint, causing him great pain and requiring an emergency trip to the doctor. When money was tight, Poppa sometimes paid the doctor with vegetables from the garden.

Although we didn't have much money, we were happy. Still, every summer, I looked longingly at the kids from away riding their beautiful, shiny bicycles. The summer kids just always seemed to have everything they wanted. I would close my eyes and imagine myself perched on the seat, handlebar streamers flapping in the breeze. I knew better than to ask for a bike, but, despite my best efforts, I am not sure how well I hid my desire. Still, there were so many things to do. We had balls and jump ropes and games for rainy days. We built secret clubhouses in the woods and played Hide and Seek and Kick the Can. In the summer, we went to the beach every day; in the winter, we skated and sledded and went to school.

On the first morning of "Scallop Week" I lay awake in bed, wriggling my toes in anticipation of a great adventure. I thought it would be fun to spend the day out on the bay instead of in school taking our usual Monday-morning spelling test. The rest of my family was not as excited. My older sister, Jen, didn't much care for the boat, and my little brother, Charlie, just wanted to stay home and play. Nevertheless, we all hurried downstairs for a hearty oatmeal breakfast at Mama's urging before racing off to the dock where Poppa kept the *Pineapple*. He loaded five bushel baskets aboard—one for each passenger—as well as lunch, sweaters, life preservers, and a rake for scalloping. The rake handle was almost twice as long as Poppa. It had to be long so he could reach deep into the water and scoop the scallops from the bottom. Some of the more experienced fishermen used other ways to catch scallops, some faster, but raking was the only way Poppa knew. Schoolteachers did not have much fishing equipment.

We climbed aboard and settled down for the short ride out onto the bay, hollering to our friends who were already at work. The harbor was full of all kinds of boats—including a few sleek sailboats and fancy cabin cruisers owned by people from away who hadn't left yet for the season. Next to them were the townsfolk's lobster boats, small fishing boats, and dinghies of every color imaginable. Everyone was taking advantage of the scallop bounty. Some of the regular fishermen wore bright yellow oilskin pants and shiny black boots to keep as dry as possible.

It was a perfect fall day, bright and crisp as a new apple, the sky so blue it almost hurt to look at it. When we reached a spot far enough away from the other boats, Poppa stopped the engine and let the boat drift. We settled down as comfortably as we could and Poppa started to work. The water was deep, and I could see it was hard work for Poppa to scratch the bottom and then raise the heavy rake, loaded with scallops, rocks, and other debris to the surface, over and over again. Each time the debris and junk had to be cleaned up and tossed overboard while the scallops were rinsed and put into the basket.

I was fascinated by the beautiful scallop shells that slowly filled our baskets. Every one seemed different, with lovely patterns of red and blue, black, and purple. Poppa told us scallops are the only mollusks that can move, and that inside their lovely shells, they have many blue eyes. Scallops were my favorite, much more interesting than clams or mussels.

By lunchtime, as we ate our thick cheese sandwiches, I had grown tired of just sitting still to stay out of the way. I thought surely we would return to shore soon. I could see Poppa was very tired and Momma rubbed his neck to help relax his aching muscles. But when the picnic things were packed away, Poppa started raking again.

To pass the time, Jen suggested we play Twenty Questions and I Spy, and then every other game we could think of. After that, we sang every song we could remember. Still Poppa raked on and on. At long last, as a fiery fall sun was setting over the coastline— and only after all five baskets were full of scallops—we headed for shore. Most of the other boats had already filled their baskets and gone home.

At the dock, we found Mr. Black waiting for us with his old red truck. He bought everyone's catch right on the spot and paid the fishermen cash. After Poppa sold his scallops, he gave Jen, Charlie, and me each a shiny quarter—he called it "patience money."

"It's a reward for a long, hard day of sitting still," he said.

On the short ride home, we spent the money many times over in our imaginations—a trip to Barney's store for Red Hots or licorice shoelaces, or perhaps root beer barrels and bubble gum. When I asked Poppa what he was going to do with his "patience money," he just said to me, "Marcie, it's for something special."

That night in bed, despite my new quarter, I grew unhappy thinking about the next day, another long, boring day of doing nothing and just staying out of the way. I wanted to skip it altogether, but in the morning, Poppa would hear of no such thing.

"Five people means five bushels," he said in a voice that meant, *Better not argue.*

Once again, Poppa did not quit until he had filled all five baskets—long after the rest of us would happily have quit and gone home. That evening Poppa showed Momma an angry bruise on his shoulder caused by the constant rubbing of the rake handle. Momma fashioned a thick pad to fit under his suspenders to protect the sore spot.

Wednesday morning dawned cool and cloudy, with a brisk fall wind coming in from the sea. I knew it would be very unpleasant on the bay. The boat would rock all day long in the waves and wind. I even thought wistfully about school. Momma packed hot soup to keep us warm, but everyone was pretty cold by the time Poppa finished. He was so cold and tired that his lips had turned gray, and he could barely lift his arm.

After three days of scalloping, I had three shiny quarters—the most money I'd ever had in my life—with the promise of three more to come. But I wondered why Poppa needed the money so badly. Why did he continue to work so hard even though he was hurting so much?

Both Thursday and Friday mornings dawned even cloudier and colder. Momma packed old blankets in with the supplies to help keep us warm, as well as some fudge, hoping to sweeten everyone's temper as another day dragged on and we grew tired of sitting. I brought along some storybooks to read aloud to Charlie. Poppa was pleased that I'd thought of Charlie's happiness because he knew it was really hard for Charlie to sit still. Momma sometimes called Charlie "little itch."

Saturday, the sixth day, was the last one for scalloping, and the pleasant, sunny morning promised a much warmer day ahead. Still, I considered pleading with Poppa to let me stay at home. I thought of how much fun I could have ashore on such a brilliant autumn day. I already had five quarters I never expected to have, and that seemed like quite enough.

"I wish I knew why Poppa needed his 'patience money,' " I said to Jen. "It must be for something really important." I decided to try to be patient for one more day.

Again, Poppa raked endlessly, looking more tired than I had ever seen him. Suddenly, he slipped on the wet deck. He threw his arms out wildly in an attempt to regain his balance and to break his fall. But as he reached out, his "tricky shoulder" acted up and dislocated. He lay on the wet deck of the boat, grabbing his shoulder, his face white with pain. I was scared to see my Poppa, who could handle any problem, suddenly so helpless.

"Marcie," said Poppa, "you'll have to take her in to the dock."

I was Poppa's summertime fishing buddy, and I loved it when he let me steer the *Pineapple*, but I had never–not once–done it without Poppa standing right behind my shoulder.

"Okay, Poppa, I'll try," I replied, though I had a lump of fear in my throat.

I was too small to reach the controls, so I pulled an old wooden milk box into position. When I stood on it, I could reach the controls and see through the windshield. Luckily, the boat was adrift, so I didn't need to pull up the anchor. I turned the key and the motor roared. I knew not to push the throttle in too far. I meant to take it slow and easy.

Now to find the channel, I thought.

Given the tide, the water was only deep enough in the channel to float our boat. At low tide, the channel was easy to see as it meandered through the exposed mudflats. And at high tide, there was enough water for the *Pineapple* to safely go anywhere in the bay. But today I faced a midtide and it was going out. The bay was dangerous because you couldn't easily distinguish between the channel and the shallow waters. If I didn't steer correctly, the boat would get stuck until the tide turned and came back in. That could take hours, and would mean Poppa would have a long, painful wait before he could get to the doctor.

Two types of buoys marked the channel—red ones called "nuns" and green ones called "cans." The channel ran between them. I soon spotted a red nun and, remembering Poppa's motto, "red right returning," I carefully steered the boat so that the nun was on my right. I'd never been so happy to see anything in my life as that red nun. I began to search for a green can so I could stay in the channel.

Lots of boats were heading toward the dock, their day's work already done. Most fishermen slow down when they pass slower or smaller boats, knowing the wake they make as they plow through the water can be dangerous. Our boat wasn't so small, but on this day, it surely was the slowest. Suddenly, a large boat roared past at full steam, its large wake rocking the *Pineapple* and knocking us about. The milk box I was standing on tipped back and forth and I struggled to stay upright. I heard Poppa groan as he tried to hold on with one hand and his shoulder slammed against the deck. I blinked back tears and fought to keep my balance.

As we moved closer to the dock, I could see that most boats were already on their moorings. The harbor looked awfully crowded. I felt like I was trying to thread a needle with a rope. As carefully as I could, and even more slowly, I steered between the other craft until, at last, we hit the dock with a mighty thump. I could barely unclench my hands from the wheel. I'd been holding on so tightly, my knuckles were white.

While Momma hurried Poppa off to the doctor, Jen and I secured the *Pineapple*. Together we lugged one of the heavy baskets up the ramp to where Mr. Black was waiting. When we told him about Poppa's shoulder, he helped us carry the rest, and then he paid us just as if we had raked the scallops ourselves.

As we stood on the dock waiting for Momma, holding Poppa's money, I was glad I hadn't begged to stay home. I had been in just the right place at the right time. When I got home and gave Poppa his money, he smiled at me wearily and said, "Thank you, Marcie. You did a good job. I'm proud of you."

I had never felt so grown up.

We were back in school on Monday, and life returned to normal. As the days passed, and with our "patience money" long since spent, Jen and I still wondered what Poppa would do with his. Maybe he would buy Momma a new Sunday coat since her old one was pretty shiny in the seat, or maybe some new winter boots, which he certainly needed. Maybe he had already used it to pay bills.

Finally, fall gave way to winter, and a few days before Christmas we hiked out into the woods to find the very best fir tree in the whole forest. On Christmas morning, we would see the tree dressed in all its glory for the first time.

We loved Christmas. Every house in town placed white candles in the windows; we went caroling, and we couldn't wait to perform in the Sunday school pageant. We didn't expect to find many gifts under our tree, though. Usually, we found a few small toys in our stockings, along with an orange and some candy canes, and some new socks and underwear. Oh, how I loved the smooth feeling of socks with no darns in the heels and the feeling of tight new elastic in my underpants. After a whole year of washing, sometimes that old elastic seemed a little risky.

Christmas morning dawned at last. Jen and I clattered down the stairs until we could see into the parlor. Poppa stood there with his coffee cup, smiling at us. I could see Charlie staring with his mouth agape, murmuring quietly, "Oh, oh, oh!" We hurried into the parlor to see why he was so excited. There, next to our tree, stood three beautiful shiny bicycles—a red one, a blue one, and a green one with training wheels. I couldn't speak.

And then I looked at the Christmas tree. This one was, indeed, the finest ever, for in addition to the lights and the tinsel and all our favorite family ornaments, Momma had painted dozens of beautiful scallop shells gold and silver. And as the tree gleamed in the early morning sunlight, I understood why Poppa had worked so long and so hard scalloping, and why he had needed his "patience money"—not for himself, but for us.

Each year when I hang those battered shells on my tree, I remember it all. Yes, the bicycle I wanted so badly has long since rusted away, but it turns out the bike wasn't the most important part of our Scallop Christmas. No; the best gift of all was realizing just how much my Poppa loved me—and that is what I will never forget.

JANE FREEBERG

Jane Freeberg lives on Georgetown Island in Midcoast Maine. She grew up in New York City and attended Adelphi University. She has lived in Maine for nearly thirty years. *The Scallop Christmas* is based on a true story told to her by her friend Marcia, who lived most of the story.

"It rattled around in my brain for 35 years, and when it came to mind, I'd think, 'That's a great story. I ought to write it down,' " she said. "I'm so glad I did."

Jane describes herself as "an enthusiastic Sunday painter" and an avid reader. She is married and has two sons and three grandchildren.

The Scallop Christmas is her first published book.

ASTRID SHECKELS

Astrid Sheckels is a native of the small farming town of Hatfield, Massachusetts.

She grew up listening to her father's and grandfather's tales, and has continued this family tradition by telling her own stories —although she tells hers visually. Through her colorful illustrations she gives a story more depth and dimension.

Astrid teaches art, is a member of The Society of Children's Book Writers and Illustrators, and is the recipient of the Archibald McLeish Prize for Art and the Medici Award in the Visual Arts.

She lives and maintains her studio in the rolling hills of Greenfield, Massachusetts, but has spent much time in her mother's homeland of Denmark. Her Scandinavian roots are evident in her fine art and illustrations.

The Scallop Christmas is her first published book.

To learn more about Astrid and her artwork, visit www.astridsheckels.com.